Best
Love Poems

Sharon Hanson

Series Editor
Jeffrey D. Wilhelm

Much thought, debate, and research went into choosing and ranking the 10 items in each book in this series. We realize that everyone has his or her own opinion of what is most significant, revolutionary, amazing, deadly, and so on. As you read, you may agree with our choices, or you may be surprised — and that's the way it should be!

Franklin Watts®

an imprint of

SCHOLASTIC

www.scholastic.com/librarypublishing

A Rubicon book published in association with Scholastic Inc.

Rubicon © 2008 Rubicon Publishing Inc.
www.rubiconpublishing.com

Associate Publishers: Kim Koh, Miriam Bardswich
Project Editor: Amy Land
Editors: Christine Boocock, Hughena Matheson
Creative Director: Jennifer Drew
Project Manager/Designer: Jeanette MacLean
Senior Graphic Designer: Gabriela Castillo
Graphic Designers: Rebecca Buchanan, Katherine Park

The publisher gratefully acknowledges the following for permission to reprint copyrighted material in this book.

Every reasonable effort has been made to trace the owners of copyrighted material and to make due acknowledgment. Any errors or omissions drawn to our attention will be gladly rectified in future editions.

"The Choice" copyright 1926, copyright renewed 1954 by Dorothy Parker, from THE PORTABLE DOROTHY PARKER by Dorothy Parker, edited by Marion Meade. Used by permission of Viking Penguin, a division of Penguin Group (USA) Inc.

"The River-Merchant's Wife: A Letter" By Ezra Pound, from PERSONAE, copyright ©1926 by Ezra Pound. Reprinted by permission of New Directions Publishing Corp.

"Oranges" from *New and Selected Poems*, copyright ©1995 by Gary Soto. Used with permission of Chronicle Books LLC, San Francisco.

"Seizure" from *Sweetbitter Love: Poems of Sappho*, 2006 Shambhala Books. Reprinted with permission of Willis Barnstone.

"Love from Ancient Greece" (excerpt) by Alix North from "Sappho, Circa 630 BC." Permission courtesy of Alexandria North.

"Funeral Blues" also known as "Stop All The Clocks" copyright 1940 & renewed 1968 by W.H. Auden, from COLLECTED POEMS by W.H. Auden. Used with permission of Random House, Inc.

"If You Forget Me" by Pablo Neruda, from THE CAPTAIN"S VERSES, copyright © 1972 by Pablo Neruda and Donald D. Walsh. Reprinted by permission of New Directions Publishing Corp.

"All You Need is Love" by Dr. Vicky Greenaway. Permission courtesy of Dr. Vicky Greenaway, Honorary Secretary the Browning Society.

Cover: All images–istockphoto, shutterstock

Library and Archives Canada Cataloguing in Publication

Hanson, Sharon
        The 10 best love poems / Sharon Hanson.

Includes index
ISBN: 978-1-55448-543-7

        1. Readers (Elementary). 2. Readers—Love poetry.

I. Title. II. Title: Ten best love poems.

PE1117.H36 2007   428.6   C2007-906863-4

1 2 3 4 5 6 7 8 9 10   10   17 16 15 14 13 12 11 10 09 08

Printed in Singapore

Contents

Introduction: Passionate Poetry 4

"The Choice" by Dorothy Parker 6

Parker tackles the age-old question of whether to fall for love or money.

**"The River-Merchant's Wife:
A Letter" by Ezra Pound** 10

Li Po's ancient Chinese text inspired Pound's heartbreaking poem of lost love.

**"Love's Philosophy"
by Percy Bysshe Shelley** 14

Nature's example of perfect love inspires this poem from the Romantic period.

**"When You are Old"
by William Butler Yeats** 18

The poet's own experiences with heartache influenced this poem about undying love.

"Oranges" by Gary Soto 22

The poet captures memories of a first love through vivid imagery and a sentimental tone.

"Seizure" by Sappho 26

We've all been "green with envy." Find out the origin of this saying in this poem from ancient Greece.

"Funeral Blues" by W. H. Auden 30

This popular poem puts into words the pain felt over the loss of a loved one.

"If You Forget Me" by Pablo Neruda 34

The famous Chilean poet has an honest approach to passionate love.

"Sonnet 29" by William Shakespeare 38

Shakespeare shows how thoughts of a loved one can magically transform a person's mood.

**"Sonnet 43"
by Elizabeth Barrett Browning** 42

Browning's real-life love affair inspired this famous love poem.

We Thought 46

What Do You Think? 47

Index 48

PASSIONATE
Poetry

At the touch of love, everyone becomes a poet.

— Plato

"I love you," is a simple sentence, but what does it mean? What is love? Throughout the ages, people have tried to answer these questions. Poets have explored these questions in love poems. And it's not just poets who are inspired by love. This feeling can also inspire ordinary people to speak like poets.

More than 2,000 years ago, Plato, a Greek philosopher, saw the link between love and poetry. As you can see in the quote above, Plato realized that love stirs powerful emotions. Thousands of love poems have been written since the earliest of days. Some poems express the joy love brings. Others explore the desolation of heartbreak. Poetry can help explain the beauty, passion, agony, and mystery of love.

So, how did we pick the 10 best love poems for this book? We read poems, both ancient and recent, and narrowed them down based on these criteria: We chose poems that showed intense feeling or strong emotion. The poets who wrote these works moved us with powerful words and strong concrete images. They avoided clichés, or overused expressions. These poems have a strong impact on readers. They are found in many anthologies of poems. They are read, studied, and often quoted. Some of the poems we selected were written centuries ago. And, they have endured!

Turn the page and allow your emotions to run wild. As you read these poems, decide for yourself:

desolation: *sadness; devastation*
concrete: *precise; easy for the reader to visualize*

Which is the best love poem?

The Choice

He'd have given me rolling lands,
   Houses of marble, and billowing farms,
Pearls, to trickle between my hands,
   Smoldering rubies, to circle my arms.
You — you'd only a lilting song,
   Only a melody, happy and high,
You were sudden and swift and strong —
   Never a thought for another had I.

He'd have given me laces rare,
   Dresses that glimmered with frosty sheen,
Shining ribbons to wrap my hair,
   Horses to draw me, as fine as a queen.
You — you'd only to whistle low,
   Gayly I followed wherever you led.
I took you, and I let him go —
   Somebody ought to examine my head!

— Dorothy Parker

billowing: rolling
smoldering: slow-burning
lilting: cheerful; light
gayly: happily

POET: Writer Dorothy Parker (1893–1967) was a legendary American literary figure.

BACKDROP: New York City in the Roaring Twenties was Parker's home when she wrote this classic.

POETRY: This poem was written in 1926. By this time, Parker was already a well-known writer, theater critic, and poet.

This 1926 poem asks the age-old question, love or money? Dorothy Parker wasn't the first to ask this question, and she definitely wasn't the last! In 1964, The Beatles had a hit with "Can't Buy Me Love." The 1987 movie of the same name also helped to show that money doesn't count when it comes to love.

Parker's speaker loves without avarice. The speaker in a poem isn't necessarily the poet. In poetry, the speaker is the narrative voice. This is the person the reader is supposed to imagine is talking. Parker's speaker chooses love over money. She picks the man with only a song, not the one who can give her pearls, rubies, houses, and more.

avarice: *strong greed for riches*

? The Roaring Twenties was a decade of glamour, luxury, and progress in America. How might this atmosphere have influenced Dorothy Parker's writing?

The Choice

THE CHOICE

ABOUT THE LINES

On the one hand, there's the rich man who could lavish the speaker with gifts. On the other, is the man who is "sudden and swift and strong." By the end of the last verse, the speaker has made her choice. "I took you, and I let him go," she says. But in the final line, the speaker hints that it might have been crazy to let all those riches slip away. Maybe she's not so sure after all!

? This poem suggests that the speaker is having second thoughts. Explain why you think she did or didn't make the right choice.

BETWEEN THE LINES

"The Choice" is written in light verse. Light verse is meant to be playful, simple, and funny. This poem was one of the first poems in light verse that Parker ever published. She became very well-known for writing in this style. "The Choice" is also written in tetrameter. This means that each line of the poem has four metrical feet. Each foot is a group of two or three syllables. A poem's rhythm is determined by these groupings of syllables.

lavish: *give generously*

BEHIND THE LINES

Born in New Jersey in 1893, Parker became famous writing for *Vogue*, *The New Yorker*, and other publications. She was a drama critic (the first female drama critic on Broadway!) and also wrote poetry, screenplays, and short stories. Two of her screenplays were nominated for Academy Awards in Hollywood. Thanks to her way with words, Parker became known for her witty, sarcastic, observant, and honest writing. She died of a heart attack in 1967 when she was 73.

Quick Fact

Parker wrote her last published poem in 1944. "My verses are no … good," she once said. "Let's face it honey, my verse is terribly dated."

? When Parker used the word "dated," she meant that she felt her poems were old-fashioned and out-of-date. Do you think "The Choice" is dated? Explain.

Dorothy Parker in a photo from 1948

The Expert Says…

" [The speaker] laments how she closed the door on wealth as she opened the door to romance. Like most people, she experiences mixed feelings when forced to make a choice. "

— Susan Reuling Furness, counselor, consultant, and certified poetry therapist

laments: *expresses sorrow*

10

9   8   7   6

Poetry PRIMER

When you play a game or sport, you learn the rules. In the same way, to best appreciate poetry, it helps to learn some of the basic techniques poets use. Learn about some common poetic devices in this chart.

TERM	DEFINITION	EXAMPLE
Metrical Foot	A group of two or three syllables that form the poem's beat or rhythm	"SHIN ing/RIB bons/ to WRAP/my HAIR." — Dorothy Parker
Rhyme	Use of the same sounds at the end of lines	The rhyme pattern of Parker's poem is *abab, cdcd*. This means that the first line rhymes with the third, the second with the fourth, and so on.
Simile	A comparison, using "like" or "as," between two different objects with some point in common	"Love comforts like sunshine after rain." — William Shakespeare
Metaphor	A comparison, without using "like" or "as," between two different objects with some point in common	"Life is a barren field" — Langston Hughes
Hyperbole	An exaggeration	"I'll love you dear/Till China and Africa meet/ And the river jumps over the mountain." — W. H. Auden

Quick Fact

On August 22, 1992, a 29¢ postage stamp with Dorothy Parker's picture was issued by the United States Postal Service. This date would have been Parker's 99th birthday.

Take Note

This original poem by one of America's most famous 20th-century poets ranks #10. At its core is the age-old choice between someone who has money and someone who doesn't. Parker never writes the words "money" or "love," yet the reader knows exactly what is going on. Parker creates strong concrete images to clearly explain the speaker's internal conflict.

• This poem presents love as a choice. Explain whether you think people have a choice in love, or whether people fall in love without choosing.

5   4   3   2   1

The River-Merchant's Wife: A Letter

While my hair was still cut straight across my forehead
I played about the front gate, pulling flowers.
You came by on bamboo stilts, playing horse,
You walked about my seat, playing with blue plums.
And we went on living in the village of Chokan:
Two small people, without dislike or suspicion.

At fourteen I married My Lord you.
I never laughed, being bashful.
Lowering my head, I looked at the wall.
Called to, a thousand times, I never looked back.

At fifteen I stopped scowling,
I desired my dust to be mingled with yours
Forever and forever and forever.
Why should I climb the lookout?

At sixteen you departed,
You went into far Ku-to-en, by the river of swirling eddies,
And you have been gone five months.
The monkeys make sorrowful noise overhead.

You dragged your feet when you went out.
By the gate now, the moss is grown, the different mosses,
Too deep to clear them away!
The leaves fall early this autumn, in wind.
The paired butterflies are already yellow with August
Over the grass in the West garden;
They hurt me. I grow older.
If you are coming down through the narrows of the river Kiang,
Please let me know beforehand,
And I will come out to meet you
As far as Cho-fo-Sa.

— Ezra Pound

---

cut straight across my forehead: *suggests
speaker had a traditional Chinese child's haircut
with straight bangs*

HANT'S WIFE: A LETTER"

ALL IMAGES–SHUTTERSTOCK, ISTOCKPHOTO

POET: Li Po (701–762) is known for his impressive imagination. Ezra Pound (1885–1972) wrote experimental, free verse poetry.

BACKDROP: Li Po was born in China. He was a nomad, or wanderer, who traveled all over the country. Pound was born in America but spent most of his life living in Europe.

POETRY: Li Po lived during the Tang Dynasty, or the "golden age" of Chinese poetry. Pound published this version when Modernist poetry was popular.

This memorable work has a long history. Originally written in the 8th century, this was one of Chinese poet Li Po's most famous works. In the poem, the speaker recalls earlier, happier times and expresses her longing for her husband, who has "been gone five months" on a journey. In the 20th century, the poem caught the attention of American Modernist poet Ezra Pound. Pound valued Chinese poetry for its powerful use of imagery. In 1915, Pound interpreted Li Po's work. His loose translation of Li Po's original poem brought this sad love story to an English-speaking audience.

Modernist: *the term describes early 20th-century poets who wrote mostly in free verse and rejected the overly flowery style of late 19th-century poetry*
imagery: *vivid language used to create clear pictures in the reader's mind*

THE RIVER-MERCHANT'S WIFE: A LETTER

ABOUT THE LINES

This poem is written in the form of a letter from a woman to her husband. She begins with a flashback to their childhood and marriage. At the beginning of the poem, the children are innocent. They play together "without dislike or suspicion." When she was 14, the girl married the boy. At 15, the speaker finally "stopped scowling" and grew to love her husband. A year later, her husband left on a journey. Now all she can do is long for his return.

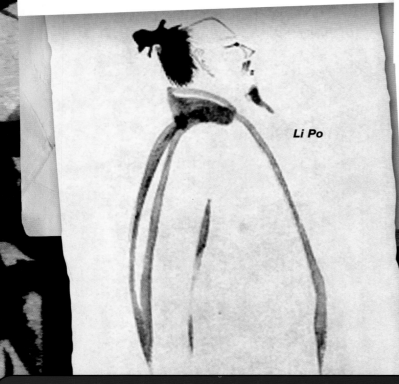

Li Po

BETWEEN THE LINES

Pound uses images to let the reader know the speaker's thoughts and feelings. After her marriage, the speaker says, " ... I looked at the wall ... I never looked back." The visual image of the wall symbolizes the barrier between childhood and adulthood. After her husband leaves, the reader senses the speaker's sadness through images of the natural world: "The monkeys make sorrowful noise overhead." Though the monkeys aren't actually sad, they sound sorrowful to the speaker because that is how she feels. Also, summer, representing youth and happiness, is slipping away. "The leaves fall early this autumn, in wind."

> **?** In this poem, images are used to show each stage of the couple's relationship. Explain which image represents each phase of the relationship.

BEHIND THE LINES

Pound's book *Cathay* included works based on classic Chinese poetry. But these were pretty far removed from the originals. Ezra Pound didn't understand Chinese. He wrote "The River-Merchant's Wife: A Letter" based on a translation of Li Po's work by a scholar named Ernest Fenollosa. Because of this, Pound's poem is called an "interpretation," not a direct translation. Pound's works aren't completely true to the original Chinese poems they're based on. However, they have allowed people who have never read Chinese poetry to at least get a glimpse at what it is all about.

The Expert Says...

" [In] *Cathay* ... [Pound] managed ... to reproduce in English not simply the meaning of the original texts but their unusual modes of feeling and perception as well. "

— Robert Kern, Associate Professor of English at Boston College and author of *Orientalism, Modernism and the American Poem*

Quick Fact

Not everyone thinks that Ezra Pound's interpretations of Chinese poetry are a good thing. Pound was accused of adding and omitting sections from Li Po's original poems. His book *Cathay* caused a lot of controversy in the poetry world.

Words with Weight

Ezra Pound once said a poet should "use no superfluous word, no adjective, which does not reveal something." This guide highlights the weight of a poet's every word.

"It is better to present one image in a lifetime than to produce voluminous works." Basically, this is how Ezra Pound felt about poetry. Pound was part of the 20th century Modernist movement in poetry. Specifically, he was very involved in Imagism. As the name suggests, this type of poetry is filled with precise visual images. Most Imagist poetry is written in free verse. Poems written in free verse don't follow traditional patterns of rhythm. They are usually without rhyme.

Pound was also greatly influenced by Chinese poetry. Chinese poetry can be challenging for Westerners to translate. Chinese characters often have several different meanings. There are also few transitions between images in a Chinese poem. This makes it hard for a translator to know how each line of a poem connects. Author Greg Whincup once said that in Chinese poetry "images are strung like jewels." The translator has to find a way to link the images with meaning.

Reading "The River-Merchant's Wife: A Letter," you get a sense of images strung together. Each set of images reveals a separate stage of the relationship between the river merchant and his wife.

superfluous: *unnecessary or needless*
voluminous: *large amounts*

Ezra Pound

Take Note

Ezra Pound's gentle poem of love and longing, based on Li Po's poem from the 8th century, takes the #9 spot. This heartfelt letter from a lonely woman to her absent husband has more impact than Dorothy Parker's lighter treatment of love in "The Choice." This poem has stirred the emotions of readers for 13 centuries.

- We know that the speaker in this poem is in love with her husband. Explain which parts of the poem show that he loves her too.

5   4   3   2   1

Love's Philosophy

The fountains mingle with the river
    And the rivers with the Ocean,
The winds of Heaven mix for ever
    With a sweet emotion;
Nothing in the world is single;
    All things by a law divine
In one spirit meet and mingle.
    Why not I with *thine*?—

See the mountains kiss high Heaven
    And the waves clasp one another;
No sister-flower would be forgiven
    If it *disdained* its brother;
And the sunlight clasps the earth,
    And the moonbeams kiss the sea:
What are all this sweet work worth
    If *thou* kiss not me?

— *Percy Bysshe Shelley*

---

thine: yours
disdained: rejected
thou: you

OSOPHY"

POET: Percy Bysshe Shelley (1792–1822) was a romantic rebel! He was a political activist and idealist, and many of his works were controversial.

BACKDROP: Shelley was born in England. He also lived in Scotland and Italy before his death in 1822.

POETRY: The English Romantic period took place around the 18th and 19th centuries. Poetry from this time focused on nature, rejected industrialization, and embraced beauty.

This poem was written by one of the most famous poets of the English Romantic period. "Love's Philosophy," in which the poet sees love and pairings in all forms of nature, is still often quoted and read at weddings. But Percy Bysshe Shelley's life wasn't all about romantic fun. At the age of 19, he was expelled from college. He then eloped with 16-year-old Harriet Westbrook. But the marriage didn't last. After Westbrook's death, Shelley married Mary Godwin. Things did not go smoothly with his children either. His son William died while very young, and at one point, some of his children were taken away by the courts and placed in foster homes.

With his troubled life, it's hard to imagine Shelley writing a sentimental love poem such as "Love's Philosophy." However, his troubles inspired his poetry. Searching for love and for answers, Shelley wrote some of history's most memorable works. He is regarded as one of the leaders of the Romantic movement.

---

eloped: *ran off to marry*

LOVE'S PHILOSOPHY

ABOUT THE LINES

In this poem, the speaker considers nature to be an example of perfect harmony. Naturally, the speaker wants to experience this sort of love! Readers get a glimpse of an early stage of the relationship between the speaker and the person he or she is talking to. The speaker's object of affection is still undecided. But the speaker presents a pretty convincing argument! Many critics believe this poem was written as a love song for Sophia Stacey. She was a young English woman with whom Shelley became friends in Italy.

BETWEEN THE LINES

This is a lyric poem, a type of poem that is often about love. Lyric poetry has a musical quality to it — many lyric poems are meant to be accompanied by music. "Love's Philosophy" has a patterned rhyme scheme, with every other line rhyming. Many critics believe that Shelley intended this poem to be a song. The poet also uses personification. This is when a poet gives human qualities to animals or objects. "[The] mountains kiss" and "the moonbeams kiss the sea" are examples of this poetic device. This makes nature come alive for the reader.

 How does personification in the poem help to portray love in a concrete way?

BEHIND THE LINES

Shelley's love poems are still remembered today, almost 200 years after they were written! But Shelley wasn't as popular during his lifetime. Many of Shelley's works caused scandals. He wrote about vegetarianism, atheism, and social justice. Many of his books, essays, and pamphlets were burned or censored. Shelley's poetry was inspired by Romanticism, by his love life, and by his radical world views.

atheism: *disbelief in the existence of any gods*
censored: *partially changed or completely banned by an authority*

Quick Fact
Shelley died shortly after his 30th birthday. He drowned when his boat, *Don Juan*, sank in a violent storm off the coast of Italy.

All in the Family

Mary Shelley

Read this account about the Shelleys to learn more about this creative couple.

Shelley's first wife, Harriet Westbrook, died in 1816. Shelley married Mary Godwin the same year. Godwin's mother, Mary Wollstonecraft, was a well-known feminist and writer. Godwin's father, William Godwin, was a journalist. It was no surprise that Mary Shelley not only married a writer but became one herself! She was only 19 when she wrote her most famous book, *Frankenstein, or the Modern Prometheus*. As legend has it, Mary Shelley wrote the book during a trip to Switzerland with her husband. The two were visiting with famous Romantic poet Lord Byron. One night, Byron suggested that each one of them should write a ghost story. Mary Shelley's was the best!

She perfected the work and published *Frankenstein* in 1818. Oddly enough, in the novel, Frankenstein isn't the name of the scary creature. In Shelley's version, Frankenstein is the last name of the scientist who creates a monster. Though she published several other novels and short stories, *Frankenstein* is Mary Shelley's most famous work.

Percy Bysshe Shelley continued to publish works up until his death in 1822. He wrote poetry, essays, and even dramas. Several of his works were published after he died. Mary Shelley edited many of these. Together, this couple produced some of the most famous works in the English language.

Percy Bysshe Shelley

The Expert Says...

"Shelley lived a life that was passionate, restless, and brief. He also left behind a remarkable body of poetry and prose."

— Theresa Kelley, Professor of English, University of Wisconsin-Madison

prose: *ordinary form of writing; written text that is not poetry*

Take Note

Shelley's passionate description of love takes the #8 spot. His vivid images of the pairing up of different things in nature help the reader understand that love is something necessary and natural. His unique description of ideal love has moved readers for over 200 years.

• The speaker's love philosophy is that all elements of nature belong in pairs. Explain how you feel about this philosophy. Did the speaker convince you? Give reasons for your answer.

5   4   3   2   1

When You are Old

When you are old and grey and full of sleep,
And nodding by the fire, take down this book,
And slowly read, and dream of the soft look
Your eyes had once, and of their shadows deep;

How many loved your moments of glad grace,
And loved your beauty with love false or true,
But one man loved the *pilgrim soul* in you,
And loves the sorrows of your changing face;

And bending down beside the glowing bars,
Murmur, a little sadly, how Love fled
And paced upon the mountains overhead
And hid his face amid a crowd of stars.

— William Butler Yeats

pilgrim soul: adventurous spirit

And nodding by the fire, take

ARE OLD"

MAUD GONNE MACBRIDE–LIBRARY OF CONGRESS; ALL OTHER IMAGES–SHUTTERSTOCK

POET: A poet and playwright, William Butler Yeats (1865–1939) was awarded the Nobel Prize in Literature in 1923.

BACKDROP: Yeats was born in Dublin, Ireland, and spent most of his life there.

POETRY: Yeats was part of the Irish Literary Revival of the late 19th and early 20th centuries. Supporters of the revival encouraged writing with traditional Irish themes, settings, and ideas.

Ever heard the saying "if you love something, set it free"? It sounds crazy to let go of something you love. But sometimes saying goodbye is the only option. "When You are Old" is a poem based on Yeats's personal experiences. He loved an Irish woman named Maud Gonne. She was a beautiful Irish actor and political activist. Yeats proposed to her several times, but she always said no. Many of Yeats's poems and plays were inspired by Gonne and by the painful fact that she didn't love him. The speaker in this poem, like Yeats himself, is a victim of unrequited love.

unrequited: *not returned*

A photo of Maud Gonne MacBride

ABOUT THE LINES

The speaker here is talking about what he predicts will happen in the future. He is sad that the love of his life doesn't love him. He talks about having left her after realizing that he cannot make her happy. But the poem is also a warning. Be careful, says the speaker, you might miss out on an amazing love! The speaker wants her to realize that he is the only person who will ever love everything about her. He warns her that in the future she will "Murmur, a little sadly, how Love fled." The speaker advises her not to reject love now, or she may regret it when she is old.

BETWEEN THE LINES

"When You are Old" is a 12-line sonnet. It is divided into three quatrains, or verses, of four lines each. Yeats uses a common rhyme scheme of *abba cddc effe*. The first line rhymes with the fourth, the second with the third, the fifth with the eighth, and so on. Yeats also uses imagery and personification. Fire here represents passion and love. The object of affection bends "down beside the glowing bars," looking for comfort and warmth. But it's too late. The speaker uses personification to give love itself human qualities. Love fled, "paced upon the mountains," and "hid his face amid a crowd of stars."

 When love is a one-way street, does it really qualify as love? What elements are missing from this kind of love?

BEHIND THE LINES

Yeats's lifelong infatuation with Maud Gonne was no secret. The two met in 1889 in Ireland. In 1902, Gonne starred in a political play written by Yeats called *Cathleen ni Houlihan*. Yeats proposed to Gonne several times, but in 1903 she married John MacBride. The marriage didn't last, and after her divorce in 1906 Yeats tried again! Gonne refused him for the last time. In 1917, Yeats married 25-year-old Georgie Hyde Lees. They were together until his death in 1939.

? In a letter to Yeats, Gonne once wrote that the "world should thank me for not marrying you." Explain what you think she meant by this.

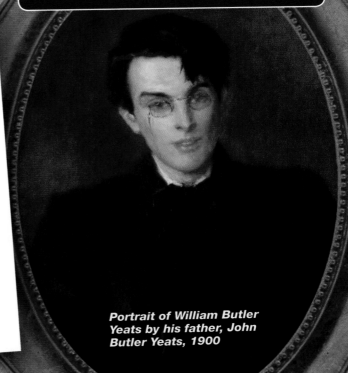

Portrait of William Butler Yeats by his father, John Butler Yeats, 1900

Quick Fact

Maud Gonne was an Irish nationalist. She wrote political articles and fought for Ireland's independence. Her son, Seán MacBride, was one of the founders of Amnesty International and won a Nobel Peace Prize in 1974.

The Expert Says...

" Yeats cannot know his love is truer than another man's, but each love is unique. No other man loved her in the way he did, even if they loved her as much. "

— Steve Stonebraker, creator of "Unrequited Love: Agony and Rapture" Web site

7

LOVE SICK

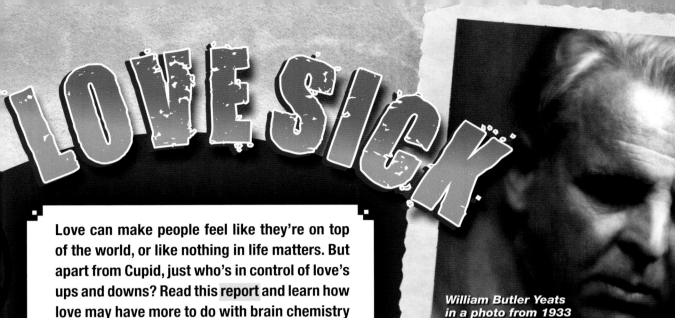

William Butler Yeats in a photo from 1933

Love can make people feel like they're on top of the world, or like nothing in life matters. But apart from Cupid, just who's in control of love's ups and downs? Read this report and learn how love may have more to do with brain chemistry than with the mere zing of heartstrings.

Today, people are eager to get to the bottom of everything. Even love has become a topic for scientists. Articles on the science of love have recently appeared in *National Geographic*, *The Economist*, and *Psychology Today*.

Scientists have discovered that people who are in love have abnormally high serotonin levels, similar to that of people who are diagnosed with obsessive-compulsive disorder, or OCD. Serotonin is a chemical in the brain that regulates moods. "Abnormal levels of serotonin are linked to obsessive thinking; I mean that's what love oftentimes is," according to *National Geographic* writer Lauren Slater.

Love can also have an effect on the brain similar to that of addictive behaviors. When singers croon "I'm addicted to love," they might not be too far off.

---

compulsive: *obsessive; overcome by the need to accomplish or do something*

Maud Gonne in a photo from 1900

? Yeats eventually married someone else, but Maud Gonne was his muse throughout his career. In your opinion, did he ever get over her?

---

muse: *source of inspiration*

Take Note

This poem takes the #7 spot. It reflects the universal topic of unrequited love and was based on the poet's own personal heartache. The speaker declares his undying love using gentle words. He also reminds his love of what she might be giving up if she lets him go. The real-life tragic romance behind this poem helps it ring true for readers.
• The speaker in this poem is looking ahead and predicting the future. Do you think this work was Yeats's last attempt to win Gonne's heart? Explain your answer.

5   4   3   2   1

ORANGES

The first time I walked
With a girl, I was twelve,
Cold, and weighted down
With two oranges in my jacket.
December. Frost cracking
Beneath my steps, my breath
Before me, then gone,
As I walked toward
Her house, the one whose
Porch light burned yellow
Night and day, in any weather.
A dog barked at me, until
She came out pulling
At her gloves, face bright
With rouge. I smiled,
Touched her shoulder, and led
Her down the street, across
A used car lot and a line
Of newly planted trees,
Until we were breathing
Before a drugstore. We
Entered, the tiny bell
Bringing a saleslady
Down a narrow aisle of goods.
I turned to the candies
Tiered like bleachers,
And asked what she wanted —
Light in her eyes, a smile
Starting at the corners

Of her mouth. I fingered
A nickel in my pocket,
And when she lifted a chocolate
That cost a dime,
I didn't say anything.
I took the nickel from
My pocket, then an orange,
And set them quietly on
The counter. When I looked up,
The lady's eyes met mine,
And held them, knowing
Very well what it was all
About.

Outside,

A few cars hissing past,
Fog hanging like old
Coats between the trees.
I took my girl's hand
In mine for two blocks,
Then released it to let
Her unwrap the chocolate.
I peeled my orange
That was so bright against
The gray of December
That, from some distance,
Someone might have thought
I was making a fire in my hands.

— Gary Soto

---

rouge: *type of makeup used to color the cheeks*
tiered: *rising in layers; stacked*

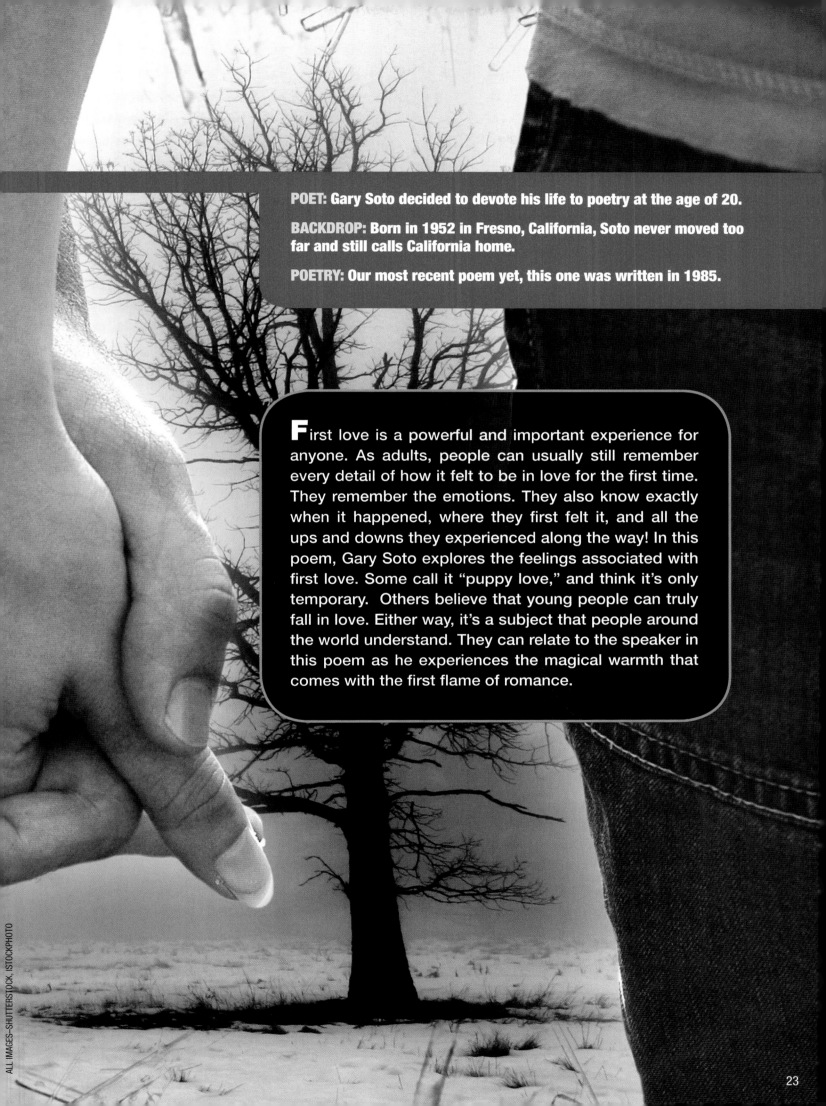

POET: Gary Soto decided to devote his life to poetry at the age of 20.

BACKDROP: Born in 1952 in Fresno, California, Soto never moved too far and still calls California home.

POETRY: Our most recent poem yet, this one was written in 1985.

First love is a powerful and important experience for anyone. As adults, people can usually still remember every detail of how it felt to be in love for the first time. They remember the emotions. They also know exactly when it happened, where they first felt it, and all the ups and downs they experienced along the way! In this poem, Gary Soto explores the feelings associated with first love. Some call it "puppy love," and think it's only temporary. Others believe that young people can truly fall in love. Either way, it's a subject that people around the world understand. They can relate to the speaker in this poem as he experiences the magical warmth that comes with the first flame of romance.

ORANGES

ABOUT THE LINES

This walk was a defining moment in the boy's journey to adulthood. He remembers all the details, from the "Frost cracking/beneath my step" to the sight of the girl's house, "the one whose/Porch light burned yellow/Night and day." At the store, he showed his maturity when, realizing he did not have enough money to pay for the chocolate the girl had chosen, he silently placed an orange beside his nickel, then looked at the lady in the store and hoped she would understand. By the end, the boy remembers he was more confident and "… took my girl's hand." Like the lady in the store, readers know that this is all about first love!

> **?** In your opinion, what is more timeless, love or friendship? Is friendship an essential part of love? Explain your answer.

The winners of the 1999 Hispanic Heritage Awards, from left, Tina Ramirez for education, Plácido Domingo for arts, Antonia Hernández for leadership, and Gary Soto for literature at the John F. Kennedy Center for the Performing Arts in Washington

The Expert Says…

> [The] word 'love' never even appears; yet, because of Soto's effective use of detail and understatement, there is no doubt that "Oranges" is a genuine love poem.
>
> — Edwin Romond, American poet, author, and English teacher

BETWEEN THE LINES

"Oranges" is a narrative poem. A narrative poem tells a story. Like a story, it also has characters, settings, and a plot. Soto uses colorful descriptions to paint a picture. The reader can see the girl's "face bright/With rouge" and the orange "so bright against/The gray of December." Soto also uses similes. "Fog hanging like old/Coats" and "candies/Tiered like bleachers" are examples of similes. He uses onomatopoeia, or words that imitate the sounds they name, like "cracking" and "hissing."

> **?** To what extent do you think most poems are autobiographical, or based on the poet's life and experiences? Do you think that the speaker and the writer are usually the same person? Explain your answer.

BEHIND THE LINES

Soto is a contemporary Mexican-American poet. Much of his work is infused with cultural references. Because of this, some people consider Soto a Chicano poet. He writes about Mexican-American influences, experiences, and challenges. But as Soto himself once said, "Even though I write a lot about life in the barrio, I am really writing about the feelings and experiences of most American kids."

Chicano: *of or relating to Mexican Americans or their culture*
barrio: *crowded inner-city area of a city, mostly inhabited by a Spanish-speaking population*

Subtle Sparks

First-time writers often think they have nothing to write about. What they don't know is that some of the world's greatest poems are about ordinary things! This report discusses how common objects can inspire moving poems.

Pablo Neruda was a famous poet from Chile. He was "the greatest poet of the 20th century in any language" according to author Gabriel García Márquez. Neruda once wrote a book called *Odes to Common Things*. Each poem in the book is about an ordinary object. There is a mouthwatering poem about a tomato. There is also a warm and fuzzy sock poem. Neruda chose to write about common objects to make his poetry simple. He wanted everyone to be able to understand his work. But the objects in his poems also represent bigger themes. Neruda praised things that people take for granted.

This helps to highlight their importance. He discussed politics, feelings, and history using common items as symbols. In Neruda's odes, common objects are symbolic of the most important things in life, such as love, birth, and even death.

Soto is no stranger to using common objects in his poems either. There are actual oranges in the poem "Oranges." The fruit, though, also symbolizes something more. Bright against the gray December day, oranges represent happiness and light. In the end, oranges are a vivid image of the fire of love that burns in the speaker's heart.

Quick Fact

Soto was inspired by poet Pablo Neruda. After reading Neruda's work, Soto said, "I was bitten … I wanted to do this thing called writing poetry."

Take Note

Soto's vivid description of a very special moment in a young man's life takes the #7 spot. Soto creates punch with a very ordinary object, an orange! By injecting bright oranges into a bleak winter scene, he paints a warm, intense picture of a first love. This powerful poem stirs the emotions more than Yeats's ode to lost love.
• Why do you think Soto wanted this poem to appeal to the reader's senses? What might this have to do with love?

5   4   3   2   1

Seizure

To me he seems like a god
as he sits facing you and
hears you near as you speak
softly and laugh

in a sweet echo that jolts
the heart in my ribs. For now
as I look at you my voice
is empty and

can say nothing as my tongue
cracks and slender fire is quick
under my skin. My eyes are dead
to light, my ears

pound, and sweat pours over me.
I convulse, greener than grass,
and feel my mind slip as I
go close to death,

yet, being poor, must suffer
everything.

— Sappho, translated by Willis Barnstone

POET: Sappho (630 – 570 B.C.) was a lyric poet. Her poems were meant to be sung, not read. She is one of the most famous female poets of ancient Greece.

BACKDROP: Sappho lived on a Greek island in the Aegean Sea.

POETRY: Sappho was composing in the 7th century B.C., during Greece's Archaic period. At this time, Greece was emerging as a place of great artistry, culture, and politics.

Have your cheeks ever flushed red from embarrassment? Have you ever had goose-bumps from something other than the cold? It's not uncommon for strong emotions to affect us in all kinds of ways. Burning jealousy is one kind of strong emotion. Thousands of years ago, Greek poet Sappho was well aware of jealousy's unhealthy nature. Today, it's common to say someone's "green with envy." Many people think Sappho was the first to describe an envious person as being green! This poem explores the ways in which our emotions can physically affect us.

Statue of Greek poet Sappho

SEIZURE

ABOUT THE LINES

This poem paints a vivid picture of a strong emotion — jealousy. The speaker loves someone who is with someone else. "[He] sits facing you and/hears you near as you speak/softly and laugh." Jealousy takes over and the speaker's emotions cause a physical reaction — a convulsion! "My eyes are dead / to light, my ears / pound, and sweat pours over me." Overwhelming jealousy causes the speaker's strong reaction.

> **?** In 1180, a monk named Andreas Capellanus wrote in *The Art of Courtly Love* that "He who is not jealous cannot love." Do you agree or disagree with this statement? Explain.

BEHIND THE LINES

Sappho was born into a noble family around 630 B.C. The family was exiled around 600 B.C. and forced to live in Sicily, Italy. Sappho was married to a wealthy businessman. In one of her poems, she also talks about her daughter. Sappho was a poet and a teacher. She was very intellectual and cultured. Most of her poetry is about love.

exiled: *sent away from its native land*

> **?** In Mary Barnard's translation of "Seizure," the first line is "He is more than a hero." There are many different translations of Sappho's work. How might a translator affect a poet's work or legacy?

BETWEEN THE LINES

Most Greek poetry before Sappho was epic poetry that recorded legends and history. When Sappho was writing, poetry was becoming more personal. Sappho came to epitomize emotional, lyrical poetry. In the line, "To me he seems like a god," the poet uses a simile. In this simile, the speaker's object of affection is compared to a supernatural being. The poet also uses very dramatic, descriptive language to show what's going on. The speaker says, "my tongue / cracks" and "I convulse" to let the reader feel exactly what he is feeling.

epic: *long narrative poem about a series of heroic acts*
epitomize: *be a typical example of*

The Expert Says...

" Sappho's poems are passionate, vehement, gorgeous, and — according to the third-century scholar Longinus — sublime. "

— Eleni Sikelianos, poet and author

vehement: *intensely emotional*

10   9   8   7   6

Love from ANCIENT GREECE

In this biography excerpt, writer Alix North tells us more about this poetic pro.

Sappho was called a lyrist because, as was the custom of the time, she wrote her poems to be performed with the accompaniment of a lyre. ... She innovated lyric poetry both in technique and style. ... She was one of the first poets to ... [describe] love and loss as it affected her personally. ...

Given the fame that her work has enjoyed, it is somewhat surprising to learn that only one of Sappho's poems is available in its entirety. ...

[All] of the rest exist as fragments of her original work. ... [Over] the centuries, from neglect, natural disasters, and possibly some censorship ... her work was lost. Late in the 19th century, however, manuscripts dating back to the eighth century A.D. were discovered in the Nile Valley. ... [Excavations] in ancient Egyptian refuse heaps unearthed a quantity of papyruses. ... Here, strips of papyrus — some containing her poetry — were found in number. These strips had been used to wrap mummies, stuff sacred animals, and wrap coffins. ...

From ancient times to today, Sappho has remained an important literary and cultural figure. ... For a woman who has been dead for over two thousand years, this is quite an achievement.

---

lyre: *stringed instrument of the harp family*
innovated: *made new; updated*
refuse: *garbage*
papyruses: *ancient documents written on paper made from papyrus plants*

Quick Fact

Only one full poem plus 189 fragments of Sappho's work exist. Twenty of these are only one word long and 13 have only two words. Thirty-three of Sappho's fragments have fewer than five words, and 59 have less than 10 words!

Sappho and Alcaeus of Mytilene *by Lawrence Alma-Tadema (1881)*

Take Note

Sappho's vivid and highly emotional lines boost her lyric into the #5 spot. This love poem is all about wanting what you can't have. The reader understands the emotion because of the precise descriptions of a physical reaction. Thousands of years have not weakened the poem's powerful impact! Its intensity and lasting reputation boost it higher than Soto's poem.
• The word "jealousy" is never mentioned in this poem. Why might leaving out the obvious make the poem more effective?

5   4   3   2   1

4 "FUNERAL BL

Funeral Blues

Stop all the clocks, cut off the telephone,
Prevent the dog from barking with a juicy bone,
Silence the pianos and with muffled drum
Bring out the coffin, let the mourners come.

Let aeroplanes circle moaning overhead
Scribbling on the sky the message He Is Dead,
Put crepe bows round the white necks of the public doves,
Let the traffic policemen wear black cotton gloves.

He was my North, my South, my East and West,
My working week and my Sunday rest,
My noon, my midnight, my talk, my song;
I thought that love would last for ever: I was wrong.

The stars are not wanted now: put out every one;
Pack up the moon and dismantle the sun;
Pour away the ocean and sweep up the wood.
For nothing now can ever come to any good.
— W. H. Auden

crepe: *lightweight fabric with a finely crinkled surface*

UES"

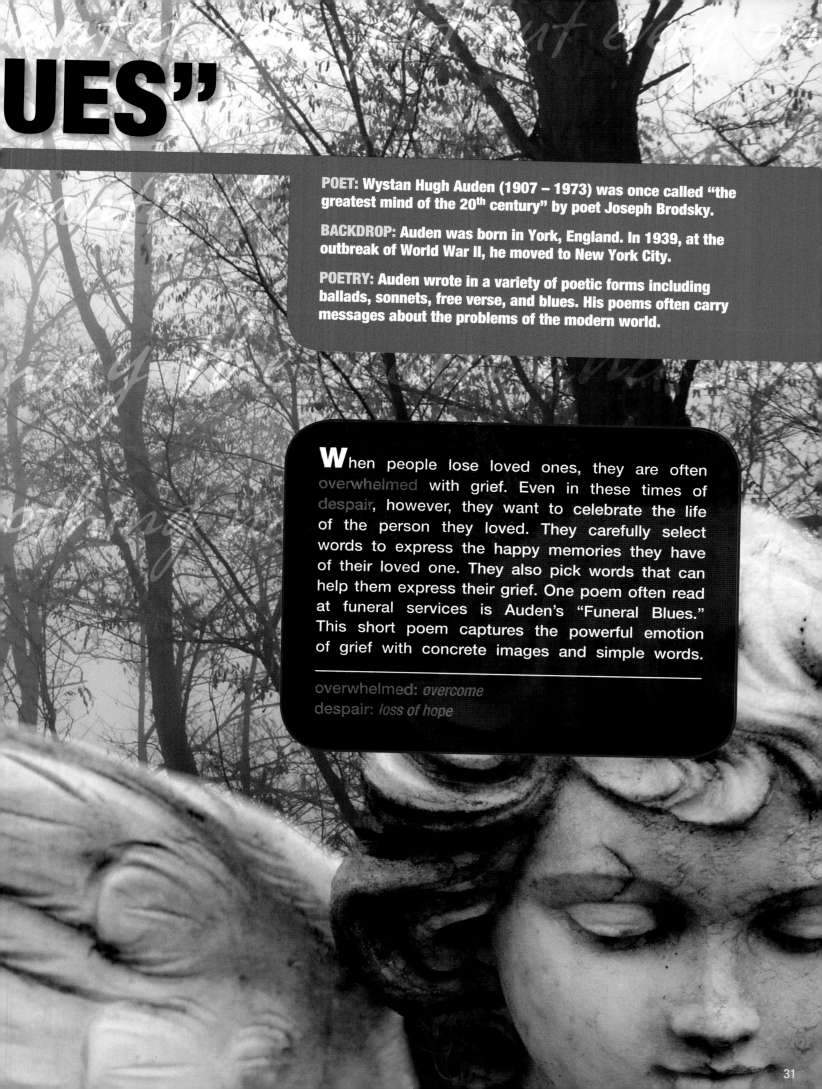

POET: Wystan Hugh Auden (1907 – 1973) was once called "the greatest mind of the 20th century" by poet Joseph Brodsky.

BACKDROP: Auden was born in York, England. In 1939, at the outbreak of World War II, he moved to New York City.

POETRY: Auden wrote in a variety of poetic forms including ballads, sonnets, free verse, and blues. His poems often carry messages about the problems of the modern world.

When people lose loved ones, they are often overwhelmed with grief. Even in these times of despair, however, they want to celebrate the life of the person they loved. They carefully select words to express the happy memories they have of their loved one. They also pick words that can help them express their grief. One poem often read at funeral services is Auden's "Funeral Blues." This short poem captures the powerful emotion of grief with concrete images and simple words.

_____

overwhelmed: *overcome*
despair: *loss of hope*

FUNERAL BLUES

ABOUT THE LINES

With the death of a loved one, life seems over for the speaker in this poem. The speaker feels the entire world should stop as well. From now on, everything should only grieve the death of the speaker's loved one. Everyday necessities such as clocks and telephones are no longer needed. Airplanes should "scribble on the sky the message He Is Dead." Police, wearing black gloves, should announce the death to the passing traffic. Without the loved one, the whole universe, including the stars, moon, and the sun, is useless.

> The line "Prevent the dog … with a juicy bone" suggests a less serious tone. Some believe Auden is making fun of funeral elegies. Can a poem be interpreted in several ways? Do you think the poet and the reader might read different things into a poem? Explain.
>
> elegies: *songs of sorrow for the dead*

BETWEEN THE LINES

Auden builds up the grief, starting with the speaker's own immediate world, moving to the world outside the speaker's home, and then in the final verse, expanding the speaker's grief to include the universe of sun, moon, and stars. In poetry, this technique is called hyperbole, or exaggeration. Poets use this technique to emphasize a point. To make the poem musical, Auden uses a rhyme pattern of *aabb*. The first and second lines rhyme, the third and fourth, and so on.

BEHIND THE LINES

Auden felt poetry was first and foremost music. In fact, "Funeral Blues" was originally written in 1936 as a song for a play called *The Ascent of F6*. This is a play about a mountain climber trying to make his way to the peak of a mountain. Auden also included the poem in a collection called *Another Time*. Auden died in 1973. "Funeral Blues" is so famous that it has helped the sale of his poetry books years after his death.

> In ranking poems, whose opinion is more important, that of professionals or that of ordinary people?

W. H. Auden

The Expert Says…

" [Auden] is someone whom you don't have to translate into the present. … You read him and he's addressing who you are at almost any age, or at any time, or in any period. "

— Edward Mendelson, W. H. Auden's literary executor

executor: *person who is appointed to carry out another's will*

Poetry for the People

This report will show you how Auden's poem has found a place in the modern world.

Imagine going to a movie and then rushing out to buy a copy of a poem. No way, right? Well, that's what happened when the blockbuster *Four Weddings and a Funeral* hit theaters in 1994. John Hannah's emotional reading of "Funeral Blues" deeply touched moviegoers.

Auden's poem made headlines again in 2005. This time, it became part of a statue outside the King Baudouin Stadium in Brussels, Belgium. In 1985, the old stadium was the scene of one of the worst tragedies in sports history. Fans from England and Italy had gathered to watch an important soccer game. Their pushing and shoving caused a wall to collapse. Thirty-nine fans were killed.

To commemorate the lives of those who died, French artist Patrick Rimoux created a memorial sculpture. He built a stainless steel sundial that rises over 39 feet into the sky. Auden's "Funeral Blues" is etched around the base. "Auden's poem was selected primarily for the sense of loss it conveys," according to the designer.

"Funeral Blues" is etched around the base of this memorial statue outside the King Baudouin Stadium in Brussels. It was built in memory of those who died in a soccer riot in 1985.

In movies, at funerals and remembrance services, and on memorials, Auden's famous poem has helped people cope with loss. His poem has found its place in the real world, where poetry truly belongs.

Quick Fact

In 1948, Auden received the Pulitzer Prize, America's top award for writers, for his book-length poem *The Age of Anxiety*.

Take Note

"Funeral Blues" takes the #4 spot. Auden expresses grief — a powerful, universal emotion — with simple words and recognizable images. This famous poem ranks higher than Sappho's lesser known work.
- This poem is about the love the speaker feels for a lost friend or family member. Do you think it's a strange choice for a book about love poems? What does this poem say about love? Why is it so powerful?

5　　4　　3　　2　　1

If You Forget Me

I want you to know
one thing.

You know how this is:
if I look
at the crystal moon, at the red branch
of the slow autumn at my window,
if I touch
near the fire
the impalpable ash
or the wrinkled body of the log,
everything carries me to you,
as if everything that exists,
aromas, light, metals,
were little boats
that sail
toward those isles of yours that wait for me.

Well, now,
if little by little you stop loving me
I shall stop loving you little by little.

If suddenly
you forget me
do not look for me,
for I shall already have forgotten you.

If you think it long and mad,
the wind of banners
that passes through my life,
and you decide
to leave me at the shore
of the heart where I have roots,
remember
that on that day,
at that hour,
I shall lift my arms
and my roots will set off
to seek another land.

But
if each day,
each hour,
you feel that you are destined for me
with implacable sweetness,
if each day a flower
climbs up to your lips to seek me,
ah my love, ah my own,
in me all that fire is repeated,
in me nothing is extinguished or forgotten,
my love feeds on your love, beloved,
and as long as you live it will be in your arms
without leaving mine.

impalpable: impossible to feel; very fine
implacable: relentless

— Pablo Neruda, translated
by Donald D. Walsh

GET ME"

POET: Pablo Neruda (1904–1973) was a political activist and "the greatest poet of the 20th century" according to author Gabriel García Márquez.

BACKDROP: Though born in Chile, Neruda was forced to leave in 1949 because of his unpopular political beliefs. He lived in many places before he was allowed to return to Chile in 1952.

POETRY: "If You Forget Me" was published in *The Captain's Verses* in 1952. The book was dedicated by Neruda to his wife, Matilde Urrutia.

This poem first appeared as part of Pablo Neruda's famous book *The Captain's Verses*. Neruda also wrote a book called *100 Love Sonnets* for his wife, Matilde Urrutia. According to the Pablo Neruda Foundation, Urrutia was "his adulthood's great love." The sonnets were Neruda's way of recording his great love for his wife. For Neruda, poetry and love went together. This idea even inspired an Academy Award-winning movie named *Il Postino* (*The Postman*). With Madonna reading "If You Forget Me" on the movie's soundtrack, this poem reached audiences in a brand new way.

ABOUT THE LINES

The speaker here loves someone who, for now, loves him or her back. But in case something changes, the speaker gets right to the point! "[If] little by little you stop loving me/I shall stop loving you little by little." There's nothing mysterious about these lines. The speaker knows love can fade. The speaker is passionate for his or her love. But at the same time, the speaker is realistic. Love requires two people. As the speaker says, "my love feeds on your love."

Quick Fact
Pablo Neruda was just 13 when his first poem was published!

BETWEEN THE LINES

Neruda repeats the word "if" eight times. This suggests how quickly love can change. The speaker says a lover's passion can die and "leave me at the shore of the heart where I have roots." Here, Neruda, a master of metaphor, writes about elements in nature, like "shore" and "roots," to talk about a relationship between two people. In the second verse, everything reminds the speaker of the object of affection in one way or another. These metaphors creatively say, "You are always on my mind."

Neruda also uses line breaks in an interesting way. In poetry, line breaks are used to create rhythm and mood. They sometimes make certain words stand out. They can even be used to make a poem look a certain way. The first two lines are "I want you to know/one thing." If Neruda had been writing a novel, these two lines would have appeared together. Here, they are split to make "one thing" stand out.

How might this poem be different if Neruda had put the line breaks in different places? How does each line break affect how you read the poem?

Quick Fact
Born Ricardo Eliecer Neftalí Reyes Basoalto, this poet adopted the name Pablo Neruda. This was in memory of Czech poet Jan Neruda. This pen name became his legal name in 1946.

BEHIND THE LINES

Neruda published several poems while still in high school. In 1923, he published his first book, *Crepusculario*. Neruda continued to publish throughout the 1920s. His fame grew, but he didn't earn enough money writing poetry to support himself. Because of this, Neruda also worked as a diplomat. In 1934, Neruda was sent to Spain. He worked as the Chilean consul in Barcelona. In 1945, Neruda joined the Chilean Communist Party and was forced to escape to Argentina. By this time, he had published his most famous works. He had also become a well-known political activist. In 1949, he met the Chilean singer Matilde Urrutia. They were married in 1955.

consul: *official appointed by a government to look after its interests in another country*
Communist: *person who supports communism, a system in which goods are owned in common and are available to all as needed*

Quick Fact
In 1971, Neruda received the Nobel Prize in Literature. This is the world's top award for a writer.

The Expert Says...

"Neruda remains an immense presence in poetry. … He was a poet of freedom and the sea, a wondrous love poet.

— Edward Hirsch, American poet and author

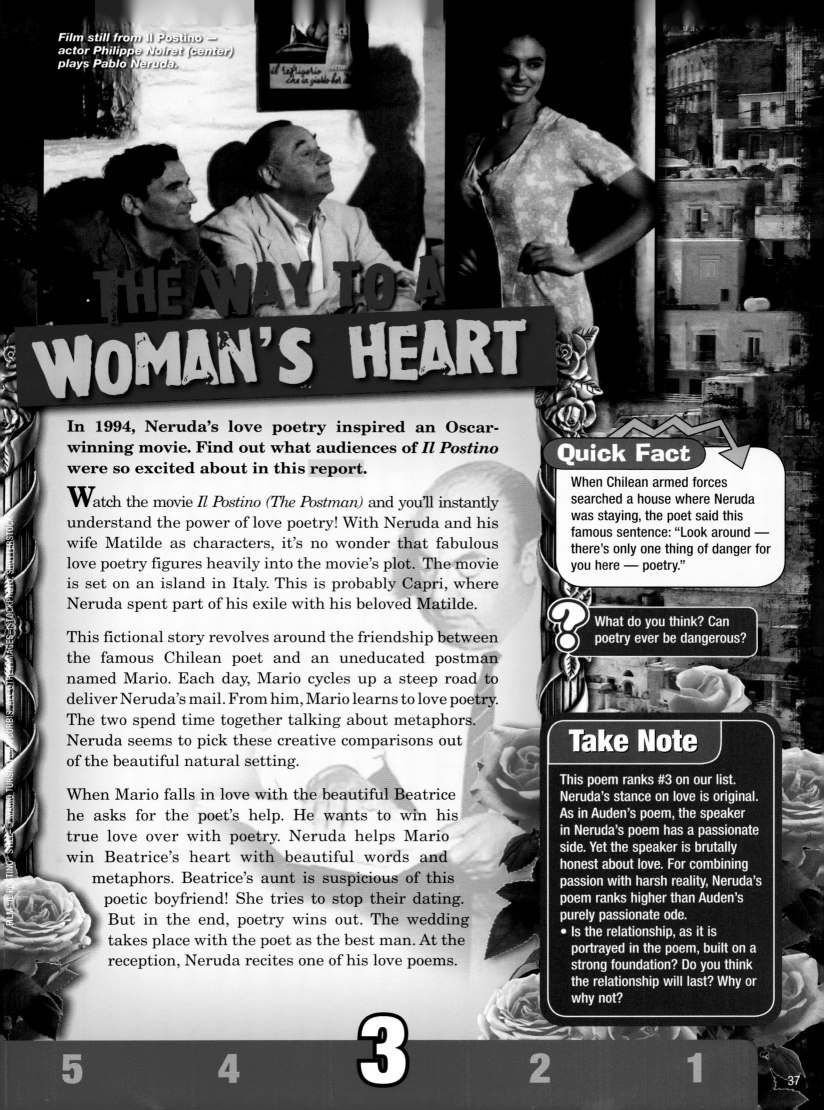

Film still from Il Postino —
actor Philippe Noiret (center)
plays Pablo Neruda.

THE WAY TO A WOMAN'S HEART

In 1994, Neruda's love poetry inspired an Oscar-winning movie. Find out what audiences of *Il Postino* were so excited about in this report.

Watch the movie *Il Postino (The Postman)* and you'll instantly understand the power of love poetry! With Neruda and his wife Matilde as characters, it's no wonder that fabulous love poetry figures heavily into the movie's plot. The movie is set on an island in Italy. This is probably Capri, where Neruda spent part of his exile with his beloved Matilde.

This fictional story revolves around the friendship between the famous Chilean poet and an uneducated postman named Mario. Each day, Mario cycles up a steep road to deliver Neruda's mail. From him, Mario learns to love poetry. The two spend time together talking about metaphors. Neruda seems to pick these creative comparisons out of the beautiful natural setting.

When Mario falls in love with the beautiful Beatrice he asks for the poet's help. He wants to win his true love over with poetry. Neruda helps Mario win Beatrice's heart with beautiful words and metaphors. Beatrice's aunt is suspicious of this poetic boyfriend! She tries to stop their dating. But in the end, poetry wins out. The wedding takes place with the poet as the best man. At the reception, Neruda recites one of his love poems.

Quick Fact

When Chilean armed forces searched a house where Neruda was staying, the poet said this famous sentence: "Look around — there's only one thing of danger for you here — poetry."

? What do you think? Can poetry ever be dangerous?

Take Note

This poem ranks #3 on our list. Neruda's stance on love is original. As in Auden's poem, the speaker in Neruda's poem has a passionate side. Yet the speaker is brutally honest about love. For combining passion with harsh reality, Neruda's poem ranks higher than Auden's purely passionate ode.
- Is the relationship, as it is portrayed in the poem, built on a strong foundation? Do you think the relationship will last? Why or why not?

5   4   **3**   2   1

Sonnet 29

When in disgrace with fortune and men's eyes,
I all alone *beweep* my outcast state,
And trouble deaf heaven with my *bootless* cries,
And look upon myself, and curse my fate,
Wishing me like to one more rich in hope,
Featured like him, like him with friends possessed,
Desiring this man's art, and that man's *scope*,
With what I most enjoy contented least;
Yet in these thoughts myself almost despising,
Haply I think on thee, and then my state,
Like to the lark at break of day arising
From sullen earth, sings hymns at heaven's gate;
For thy sweet love remembered such wealth brings
That then I scorn to change my state with kings.

— William Shakespeare

beweep: cry about
bootless: useless
scope: intelligence; range of knowledge
Haply: old-fashioned way to say "happily"

POET: William Shakespeare (1564 – 1616) was an actor, an author, a playwright, and a poet. He is one of the most famous writers of all time.

BACKDROP: Shakespeare was born in Stratford-upon-Avon, England. He moved to London, where he wrote his famous 154 sonnets.

POETRY: Shakespeare's sonnets were first published in 1609.

Think of a time when you felt really down. Was there ever a day when you compared yourself to others and felt miserable? Did everyone seem better looking or smarter than you? Did they seem more popular? It may be hard to believe, but the famous William Shakespeare had those days, too! He recorded his feelings in famous works like this one. In "Sonnet 29," Shakespeare's speaker starts off totally depressed. The speaker feels miserable and wishes to be someone else. Suddenly, the speaker thinks of his or her loved one and immediately feels better.

In this poem, Shakespeare explains the power of love in a way that even a 21st-century person can understand. This universal, timeless definition of love is just one reason why Shakespeare's works are read, studied, and loved, more than 400 years after his death.

SONNET 29

ABOUT THE LINES

The speaker is having a really bad day! Compared to others, the speaker in this poem feels ugly, untalented, and friendless. Then he or she remembers a loved one. That love changes everything! Suddenly, the speaker is as happy as a lark! In fact, the love makes the speaker feel so happy, he or she would not change places with anyone — even a king.

Quick Fact

Shakespeare turned to writing poetry when the playhouses in London closed in 1592 because of the plague.

BETWEEN THE LINES

Songs and poems are all about rhythm. The rhythm should suit the message. Shakespeare knew that. A sonnet is a 14-line poem with a specific rhyme scheme. Despite this short format, Shakespeare still creates a rhythm to suit his message. The first eight lines (octave) seem heavy and move slowly. This captures the speaker's depressed mental state. In the last six lines (sestet) the rhythm changes. No longer heavy and slow-moving, it becomes light and fast-moving. The upbeat pace reflects the speaker's upbeat mood.

Quick Fact

The rhyme scheme used in this poem is *abab cdcd efef gg*. This is called Shakespearean rhyme scheme because he made it famous.

BEHIND THE LINES

Shakespeare's 154 sonnets are some of his most famous works. They are about love, beauty, life, and growing old. When he says, "thee" and "thy," words for "you," no one knows exactly who Shakespeare means. We will never know whether his poems are autobiographical. However, the messages in his poems have lasted for centuries despite our lack of details about his personal life.

? Does knowing the personal life of the poet help in our interpretation of poetry? Why or why not?

The Expert Says...

" [Shakespeare's] sonnets are concerned entirely with love, and they run the full gamut of this universal emotion from tenderness and passion to bitterness and despair. "

— *Love Poems and Sonnets of William Shakespeare*

gamut: *entire scale or range*

The cottage in Stratford-upon-Avon where Anne Hathaway, Shakespeare's wife, is said to have grown up.

10   9   8   7   6

Famous Love Lines

William Shakespeare

No book on love poems could be written without including at least one of Shakespeare's sonnets. He wrote the book on love! Shakespeare knew how human beings think and feel. For over 400 years, people have quoted him. It looks as though we'll keep on doing so for the next 400 because he got it right! See whether you recognize these famous love lines.

"Shall I compare thee to a summer's day?
Thou art more lovely and more temperate."

"Sonnet 18"

"Good night, Good night! Parting is such sweet sorrow
That I shall say good-night till it be morrow."

Romeo and Juliet

"Love is blind and lovers cannot see."

The Merchant of Venice

"Love sought is good, but given unsought is better."

Twelfth Night

"Did my heart love till now? Forswear it, sight!
For I ne'er saw true beauty till this night."

Romeo and Juliet

temperate: *pleasingly mild*
sought: *pursued; searched for*

Take Note

Right ahead of Neruda is England's most famous writer at #2. In his sonnet, with only 14 lines, each with only 10 syllables, Shakespeare captures the ups and downs of love. The poem has lasted 400 years! It's still one of the most popular and best-loved poems.
• In your opinion, can love conquer all? What stories, TV shows, or movies reveal the power of love?

5   4   3   **2**   1

Sonnet 43

How do I love thee? Let me count the ways.

I love thee to the depth and breadth and height

My soul can reach, when feeling out of sight

For the ends of Being and ideal Grace.

I love thee to the level of every day's

Most quiet need, by sun and candle-light.

I love thee freely, as men strive for Right;

I love thee purely, as they turn from Praise.

I love thee with the passion put to use

In my old griefs, and with my childhood's faith.

I love thee with a love I seemed to lose

With my lost saints, — I love thee with the breath,

Smiles, tears, of all my life! — and, if God choose,

I shall but love thee better after death.

— Elizabeth Barrett Browning

POET: Published by age 14, Elizabeth Barrett Browning (1806 – 1861) went on to become one of England's most famous female poets.

BACKDROP: Elizabeth Barrett was born in Durham, England. She lived in Britain until 1846 when she married poet Robert Browning in secret and moved to Italy!

POETRY: This sonnet was part of the book *Sonnets from the Portuguese*, which Elizabeth Barrett wrote before her marriage.

By the age of 39, Elizabeth Barrett was bedridden. She rarely left her father's house. But her poems caught the attention of the famous poet Robert Browning. He started writing letters to Barrett, and it didn't take long for them to fall in love! Barrett married Browning, and their relationship is one of the most famous literary romances ever. The first line of "Sonnet 43" is one of the most copied lines in the English language! Barrett's very intense portrayal of love has been copied and repeated so often that it almost seems cliché. But it was completely fresh and new in the 19th century!

cliché: *stereotyped; commonplace*

A photo of Elizabeth Barrett Browning from 1848

SONNET 43

ABOUT THE LINES

In this poem, Barrett Browning attempts to define the infinite nature of the speaker's love. The speaker loves "… to the depth and breadth and height / My soul can reach." This love cannot be restricted by any measurement. The poet also uses the metaphor of love being like a religious experience. It is greater than earthly love. The speaker loves "… with a love I seemed to lose / With my lost saints." The lost saints here are dead friends or relatives. The speaker's new, intense love has replaced the grief felt because of these deaths.

BETWEEN THE LINES

The speaker repeats the line "I love thee" nine times in the poem. Repetition helps to emphasize how strongly the speaker loves. Barrett Browning uses hyperbole when she writes "I love thee with the breath, / Smiles, tears, of all my life!" The love is so strong that it has physically and emotionally taken over the speaker. Browning also uses assonance (the repetition of vowel sounds) in lines such as "I love thee to the depth and breadth and height." Barrett Browning used assonance to help her poems flow smoothly.

Quick Fact

Elizabeth Barrett's nickname may have influenced the title of her book of sonnets. Robert Browning supposedly called her "my little Portuguese" because of her dark hair.

The Expert Says…

" Robert was completely entranced by Elizabeth. They loved each other deeply; they were absolute soulmates. "

— Sally Brown, Curator of Literary Manuscripts, British Library

BEHIND THE LINES

By the time Barrett met Browning, she was already a well-known poet. She and Browning started writing love letters to each other in 1845, but the road to happiness wasn't easy. Barrett's father didn't want any of his children to get married. He never gave his daughter his blessing. She was forced to elope with Browning. Though she was happily married until her death in 1861, Elizabeth Barrett Browning was disinherited. She never spoke to her father again after her marriage.

disinherited: *left out of a will or inheritance*

? In what ways does your knowledge of Robert Browning's and Elizabeth Barrett's difficult courtship enhance your understanding of this sonnet?

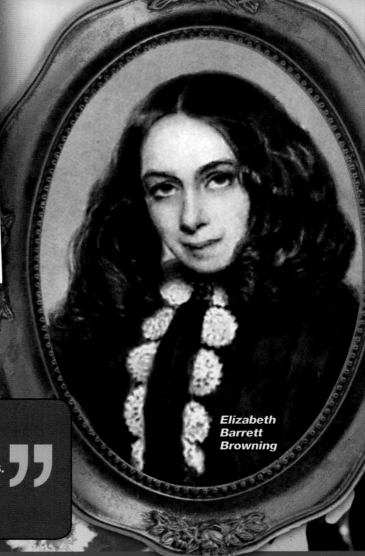

Elizabeth Barrett Browning

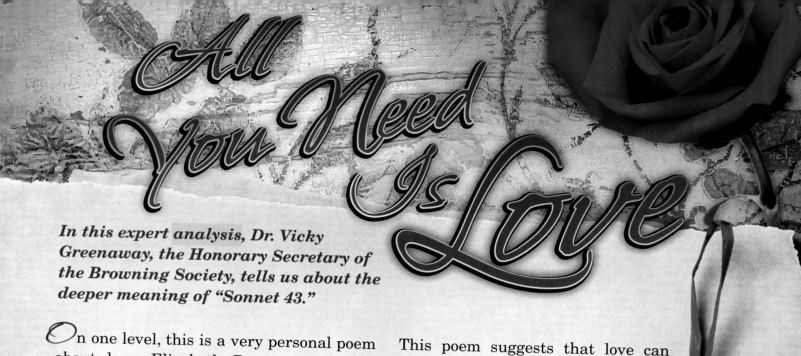

All You Need Is Love

In this expert analysis, Dr. Vicky Greenaway, the Honorary Secretary of the Browning Society, tells us about the deeper meaning of "Sonnet 43."

On one level, this is a very personal poem about love. Elizabeth Barrett wrote the poem to her soon-to-be husband, Robert Browning, during their courtship. Theirs was a great Victorian love story. It included a tyrannous father, a forbidden love, and a romantic elopement to Italy!

The poem begins as an attempt to describe love. It does so through matching love to a series of very different, contrasting experiences and emotions. In showing how love is like all of these things, it shows how love is greater than any one of them. Love is also a unifying force in this poem. The repeated line "I love thee" is a poetic device. It is used to indicate the unifying power of love. This line creates a common link between each (very different) emotion and experience discussed.

This poem suggests that love can bring unity on a wider level, too. Some of the items on the poet's list refer to political and religious struggles. The poet seems to suggest that "love," in its ability to unify, can heal these social differences and divisions as well.

In this poem, love offers meaning and resolution to the individual and to the world in general. The last line even suggests that love can heal the greatest of all man's divisions. Love can heal the division between life and death itself.

Victorian: *relating to the arts or tastes of English people during the reign of Queen Victoria*

tyrannous: *oppressive; very controlling*

Quick Fact

Elizabeth Barrett and Robert Browning exchanged 574 letters during the first 20 months of their relationship!

Take Note

Topping our list is one of Elizabeth Barrett Browning's sonnets. Emotional, beautiful, and famous, this poem has it all! Inspired by a true love story, "Sonnet 43" is one of the most copied, recited, and memorized of poems. It is considered one of the world's most famous love poems.

- In "Sonnet 43," Browning is considered to be the one talking. How might you read the poem differently if she weren't the speaker?

5   4   3   2   1

The Choice

He'd have given me rolling lands,
    Houses of marble, and billowing farms,
Pearls, to trickle between my hands,
    Smoldering rubies, to circle my arms.
You — you'd only a lilting song,
    Only a melody, happy and high,
You were sudden and swift and strong —
    Never a thought for another had I.

He'd have given me laces rare,
    Dresses that glimmered with frosty sheen,
Shining ribbons to wrap my hair,
    Horses to draw me, as fine as a queen.
You — you'd only to whistle low,
    Gayly I followed wherever you led.
I took you, and I let him go —
    Somebody ought to examine my head!

— Dorothy Parker

The River-Merchant's Wife: A Letter

While my hair was still cut straight across my forehead
I played about the front gate, pulling flowers.
You came by on bamboo stilts, playing horse,
You walked about my seat, playing with blue plums.
And we went on living in the village of Chokan:
Two small people, without dislike or suspicion.

At fourteen I married My Lord you.
I never laughed, being bashful.
Lowering my head, I looked at the wall.
Called to, a thousand times, I never looked back.

At fifteen I stopped scowling,
I desired my dust to be mingled with yours
Forever and forever and forever.
Why should I climb the lookout?

At sixteen you departed,
You went into far Ku-to-en, by the river of swirling eddies,
And you have been gone five months.
The monkeys make sorrowful noise overhead.

You dragged your feet when you went out.
By the gate now, the moss is grown, the different mosses,
Too deep to clear them away!
The leaves fall early this autumn, in wind.
The paired butterflies are already yellow with August
Over the grass in the West garden;
They hurt me. I grow older.
If you are coming down through the narrows of the river Kiang,
Please let me know beforehand,
And I will come out to meet you
As far as Cho-fo-Sa.

— Ezra Pound

ORANGES

The first time I walked
With a girl, I was twelve,
Cold, and weighted down
With two oranges in my jacket.
December. Frost cracking
Beneath my steps, my breath
Before me, then gone,
As I walked toward
Her house, the one whose
Porch light burned yellow
Night and day, in any weather.
A dog barked at me, until
She came out pulling
At her gloves, face bright
With rouge. I smiled,
Touched her shoulder, and led
Her down the street, across
A used car lot and a line
Of newly planted trees,
Until we were breathing
Before a drugstore. We
Entered, the tiny bell
Bringing a saleslady
Down a narrow aisle of goods.
I turned to the candies
Tiered like bleachers,
And asked what she wanted —
Light in her eyes, a smile
Starting at the corners

Of her mouth. I fingered
A nickel in my pocket,
And when she lifted a chocolate
That cost a dime,
I didn't say anything.
I took the nickel from
My pocket, then an orange,
And set them quietly on
The counter. When I looked up,
The lady's eyes met mine,
And held them, knowing
Very well what it was all
About.

Outside,
A few cars hissing past,
Fog hanging like old
Coats between the trees.
I took my girl's hand
In mine for two blocks,
Then released it to let
Her unwrap the chocolate.
I peeled my orange
That was so bright against
The gray of December
That, from some distance,
Someone might have thought
I was making a fire in my hands.

— Gary Soto

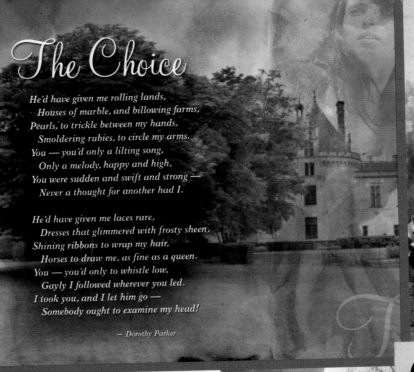

We Thought …

Here are the criteria we used in ranking the 10 best love poems.

The love poem:
- Was totally original when written
- Helps the reader gain a better understanding of love
- Explores love's most puzzling characteristics
- Uses interesting poetic devices
- Uses concrete language to illustrate love
- Is renowned as a famous love poem
- Moves the reader emotionally

Funeral Blues

Stop all the clocks, cut off the telephone,
Prevent the dog from barking with a juicy bone,
Silence the pianos and with muffled drum
Bring out the coffin, let the mourners come.

Let aeroplanes circle moaning overhead
Scribbling on the sky the message He Is Dead,
Put crepe bows round the white necks of the public doves,
Let the traffic policemen wear black cotton gloves.

He was my North, my South, my East and West,
My working week and my Sunday rest,
My noon, my midnight, my talk, my song;
I thought that love would last for ever: I was wrong.

The stars are not wanted now: put out every one;
Pack up the moon and dismantle the sun;
Pour away the ocean and sweep up the wood.
For nothing now can ever come to any good.

— W. H. Auden

If You Forget Me

I want you to know
one thing.

You know how this is:
if I look
at the crystal moon, at the red branch
of the slow autumn at my window,
if I touch
near the fire
the impalpable ash
or the wrinkled body of the log,
everything carries me to you,
as if everything that exists,
aromas, light, metals,
were little boats
that sail
toward those isles of yours that wait for me.

Well, now,
if little by little you stop loving me
I shall stop loving you little by little.

If suddenly
you forget me
do not look for me,
for I shall already have forgotten you.

If you think it long and mad,
the wind of banners
that passes through my life,
and you decide
to leave me at the shore
of the heart where I have roots,
remember
that on that day,
at that hour,
I shall lift my arms
and my roots will set off
to seek another land.

But
if each day,
each hour,
you feel that you are destined for me
with implacable sweetness,
if each day a flower
climbs up to your lips to seek me,
ah my love, ah my own,
in me all that fire is repeated,
in me nothing is extinguished or forgotten,
my love feeds on your love, beloved,
and as long as you live it will be in your arms
without leaving mine.

Pablo Neruda

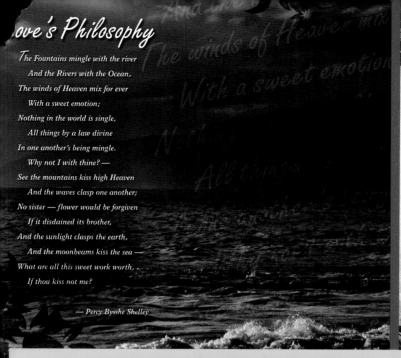

ove's Philosophy

The Fountains mingle with the river
    And the Rivers with the Ocean,
The winds of Heaven mix for ever
    With a sweet emotion;
Nothing in the world is single,
    All things by a law divine
In one another's being mingle.
    Why not I with thine? —
See the mountains kiss high Heaven
    And the waves clasp one another;
No sister — flower would be forgiven
    If it disdained its brother,
And the sunlight clasps the earth,
    And the moonbeams kiss the sea —
What are all this sweet work worth,
    If thou kiss not me?

— Percy Bysshe Shelley

When You are Old

When you are old and grey and full of sleep,
And nodding by the fire, take down this book,
And slowly read, and dream of the soft look
Your eyes had once, and of their shadows deep;

How many loved your moments of glad grace,
And loved your beauty with love false or true,
But one man loved the pilgrim soul in you,
And loves the sorrows of your changing face;

And bending down beside the glowing bars,
Murmur, a little sadly, how Love fled
And paced upon the mountains overhead
And hid his face amid a crowd of stars.

— William Butler Yeats

What Do You Think?

1. Do you agree with our ranking? If you don't, try ranking these love poems yourself. Justify your ranking with data from your own research and reasoning. You may refer to our criteria, or you may want to draw up your own list of criteria.

2. Here are three other love poems that we considered but in the end did not include in our top 10 list: "Annabel Lee" by Edgar Allan Poe, "Heart, we will forget him!" by Emily Dickinson, and "She Walks in Beauty" by George Gordon Byron.
   • Find out more about these love poems. Do you think they should have made our list? Give reasons for your response.
   • Are there other love poems that you think should have made our list? Explain your choices.

Seizure

To me he seems like a god
as he sits facing you and
hears you near as you speak
softly and laugh

in a sweet echo that jolts
the heart in my ribs. For now
as I look at you my voice
is empty and

can say nothing as my tongue
cracks and slender fire is quick
under my skin. My eyes are dead
to light, my ears

pound, and sweat pours over me.
I convulse, greener than grass,
and feel my mind slip as I
go close to death,

yet, being poor, must suffer
everything.

— Sappho, translated by Willis Barnstone

Sonnet 29

When in disgrace with fortune and men's eyes,
I all alone beweep my outcast state,
And trouble deaf heaven with my bootless cries,
And look upon myself, and curse my fate,
Wishing me like to one more rich in hope,
Featured like him, like him with friends possessed,
Desiring this man's art, and that man's scope,
With what I most enjoy contented least;
Yet in these thoughts myself almost despising,
Haply I think on thee, and then my state,
Like to the lark at break of day arising
From sullen earth, sings hymns at heaven's gate;
For thy sweet love remembered such wealth brings
That then I scorn to change my state with kings.

— William Shakespeare

Sonnet 43

How do I love thee? Let me count the ways.
I love thee to the depth and breadth and height
My soul can reach, when feeling out of sight
For the ends of Being and ideal Grace.
I love thee to the level of every day's
Most quiet need, by sun and candle-light.
I love thee freely, as men strive for Right;
I love thee purely, as they turn from Praise.
I love thee with the passion put to use
In my old griefs, and with my childhood's faith.
I love thee with a love I seemed to lose
With my lost saints, — I love thee with the breath,
Smiles, tears, of all my life! — and, if God choose,
I shall but love thee better after death.

— Elizabeth Barrett Browning

Index

A

Annabel Lee, 47
Art of Courtly Love, The, 28
Assonance, 44
Auden, Wystan Hugh, 9, 30–33, 37

B

Barnstone, Willis, 26
Brown, Sally, 44
Browning, Elizabeth Barrett, 42–45
Browning, Robert, 43–45
Byron, George Gordon, 17, 47

C

Capellanus, Andreas, 28
Captain's Verses, The, 35
Cathay, 12
Choice, The, 6–9, 13

D

Dickinson, Emily, 47

E

Elegies, 32

F

Fenollosa, Ernest, 12
Four Weddings and a Funeral, 33
Funeral Blues, 30–33
Furness, Susan Reuling, 8

G

Gonne, Maud, 19–21
Greenaway, Vicky, 45

H

Hathaway, Anne, 40
Heart, we will forget him!, 47
Hirsch, Edward, 36
Hughes, Langston, 9
Hyperbole, 9, 32, 44

I

If You Forget Me, 34–37
Il Postino, 35, 37
Imagery, 11, 20

K

Kelley, Theresa, 17
Kern, Robert, 12

L

Love's Philosophy, 14–17
Love Poems and Sonnets of William Shakespeare, 40
Lyric poem, 16, 27–29

M

Mendelson, Edward, 32
Merchant of Venice, The, 41
Metaphor, 9, 36–37, 44
Metrical Foot, 9
Modernist, 11, 13

N

Narrative poem, 24, 28
Neruda, Pablo, 25, 34–37, 41
Nobel Prize in Literature, 19, 36
North, Alix, 29

O

Odes to Common Things, 25
100 Love Sonnets, 35
Onomatopoeia, 24
Oranges, 22–25
Orientalism, Modernism and the American Poem, 12

P

Parker, Dorothy, 6–9, 13
Personification, 16, 20
Plato, 5
Po, Li, 11–13
Poe, Edgar Allan, 47
Poetic devices, 9, 16, 45–46
Pound, Ezra, 10–13
Pulitzer Prize, 33

R

Rhyme, 9, 13, 16, 20, 32, 40
River-Merchant's Wife: A Letter, The, 10–13
Romanticism, 16
Romeo and Juliet, 41
Romond, Edwin, 24

S

Sappho, 26–29, 33
Seizure, 26–29
Shakespeare, William, 9, 38–41
Shakespearean rhyme scheme, 40
Shelley, Mary Godwin, 15, 17
Shelley, Percy Bysshe, 14–17
She Walks in Beauty, 47
Sikelianos, Eleni, 28
Simile, 9, 24, 28
Sonnet 18, 41
Sonnet 29, 38–41
Sonnet 43, 42–45
Sonnets from the Portuguese, 43
Soto, Gary, 22–25, 29
Stonebraker, Steve, 20

T

Tetrameter, 8
Twelfth Night, 41

U

Urrutia, Matilde, 35–37

W

Walsh, Donald D., 34
When You are Old, 18–21

Y

Yeats, William Butler, 18–21, 25